FROM ASHES TO

Heiresses

A Pride and Prejudice Variation

by

Renata McMann & Summer Hanford

COPYRIGHT

Pride and Prejudice Villains Revisited – Redeemed –
Reimagined A Collection of Six Short Stories
Includes from above: *Lady Catherine Regrets, Mary Younge,
Mr. Collins' Deception* and *Caroline and the Footman,* along
with two additional flash fiction pieces, *Mrs. Bennet's Triumph*
and *Wickham's Journal.*

Georgiana's Folly & Elizabeth's Plight: Wickham Coin Series,
Volumes I & II
Includes from above: *Elizabeth's Plight* and *Georgiana's Folly.*

Pride and Prejudice Variations by Renata McMann
Why Wed?
Is Esteem Enough?
Besieged Heiresses

Heiress to Longbourn
Anne de Bourgh Manages
Three Daughters Married
The Inconsistency of Caroline Bingley
Pemberley Weddings
The above five stories are collected in:
Pride and Prejudice Variations: A Collection of Short Stories

Pride & Prejudice Variations by Summer Hanford
Dishonorable Gentlemen – Volume One of The Bennet Gang
Gentlemen of Honor – Volume Two of The Bennet Gang
Mr. Darcy's Bookshop*
The Adventures of Anne de Bourgh of Rosings v. I*
The Adventures of Anne de Bourgh of Rosings v. II*
Mr. Darcy's Matchmaker*
Once Upon a Time in Pemberley*

*available as an audio book

FROM ASHES TO
HEIRESSES

PROLOGUE

Mr. Phillips sat down at his desk to write Mr. Gardiner.

My Dear Brother Edward,

It is with great sorrow I must inform you there was a fire at Longbourn. Most regretfully, it took place in the night and the entire family was abed. It can be considered a great act of fortune Jane and Elizabeth were not there, but the rest of the family perished.

Four servants escaped. Inquiries have led me to conclude the fire likely started in the parlor near the main staircase. It has come to light Lydia and Kitty were discovered experimenting with cigars near that area earlier in the evening. I would make no damning conclusions based on what little can be gleaned, but this may have started a fire that wasn't noticed until it raged out of control after everyone was settled for the night.

What I can say with moderate certainty is the servants' stairway was safe for longer than the main stairway. I may also report one of the servants who escaped heard Mrs. Bennet insisting she get her jewels. Sadly, those will be the last words any hear from our dear Mr. and Mrs. Bennet, Mary, Kitty or Lydia.

It is my understanding Jane and Elizabeth are with you in London, though planning to return soon. If this letter manages to reach you before they depart, please consider accompanying them. We will be on the lookout for them here as well. They will, of course, stay with us.

We have room for you and Mrs. Gardiner as well. I urge you to make whatever haste you can to join us here. I have a copy of Mr. Bennet's will, which names you and me as co-executors. Jane and Elizabeth will both be devastated. I believe your presence to be both necessary and helpful. The funerals will be held on Saturday.

Yours, etc.
J. Phillips

CHAPTER ONE

One Week Earlier…

Elizabeth was glad to be afforded a carriage, and a pleasant travel companion. She'd found her time in Kent interesting, to say the least, but was very eager to be reunited with Jane and to see her aunt and uncle Gardiner. She turned from the window, aware of Maria Lucas's excitement and wondering how long the girl could keep up her current level of decorum.

"Good gracious!" cried Maria, after a few minutes' silence, "it seems but a day or two since we first came! and yet how many things have happened!"

"A great many indeed," said her companion with a sigh.

"We have dined nine times at Rosings, besides drinking tea there twice! How much I shall have to tell!"

Elizabeth added privately, "And how much I shall have to conceal!"

Elizabeth was glad she had time for reflection during the journey to London, since she had much to think about. Mostly, she thought about Mr. Darcy and his abysmal proposal. Elizabeth had refused him angrily, accusing him of harming both his childhood friend, Mr. Wickham, and her sister, Jane. That very much seemed like the correct course of action at the time, especially since he'd added insult to her station and family to his already egregious crimes.

Now, when it was much too late, she realized she hadn't

behaved as well as she should have. That didn't mean she wasn't still happy to have refused him. His proposal was nothing short of insulting.

He'd subsequently written her a letter, though, much to her surprise. In that letter, he explained the truth about Mr. Wickham. He also justified his conduct regarding Jane. While Elizabeth didn't agree with his motives for separating her most beloved sister and Mr. Bingley, she could see they weren't malicious. Mr. Darcy had acted as a friend must, making the deed nearly laudable. She was glad she would never see him again, because she was embarrassed, she'd misjudged him so completely and refused him with so little consideration for his emotions or for politeness.

Their journey was performed without much conversation, or any alarm; and within four hours of their leaving Hunsford they reached Mr. Gardiner's house, where they were to remain a few days with Elizabeth's aunt, uncle, cousins and Jane.

Jane looked well, and Elizabeth had little opportunity of studying her spirits, amidst the various engagements which the kindness of her aunt had reserved for them. But Jane was to go home with her, and at Longbourn there would be leisure enough for observation.

It was not without an effort, meanwhile, that she could wait even for Longbourn, before she told her sister of Mr. Darcy's proposals. To know that she had the power of revealing what would so exceedingly astonish Jane, and must, at the same time, so highly gratify whatever of her own vanity she had not yet been able to reason away, was such a temptation to openness as nothing could have conquered but the state of indecision in which she remained as to the extent of what she should communicate; and her fear, if she once entered on the subject, of being hurried into repeating something of Bingley which might only grieve her sister further.

For they had not all been mad. Mr. Bingley had indeed been on the verge of proposing to Jane, which would have given her a supreme happiness. Mr. Darcy's letter explained why he and Bingley's sisters persuaded Mr. Bingley not to do so. Mr. Darcy sharply objected to the behavior of Jane's and Elizabeth's younger sisters and parents. Though she still decried his interference, Elizabeth could see Mr. Darcy had some justification for his actions. It grieved her that the behavior of members of their family had taken such a disastrous toll on Jane's chance of happiness with the man she loved, and who appeared to love her.

Not enough, though, clearly. How could Mr. Bingley have loved Jane enough, after all, when he'd allowed himself to be persuaded away from her? As unhappy as losing him must make her sister, Elizabeth wasn't sure Jane should be with a man who could so easily remove himself.

***

When their visit with their aunt and uncle was over, Elizabeth and Jane left London amid a sea of well wishes and invitations to return. In truth, Elizabeth was a bit sad to depart. She loved her aunt and uncle, and her cousins, very much. She missed home, though, and she would be happy for a return to normality. Perhaps once in Longbourn again, she and Jane could both put their disastrous interactions with the opposite sex behind them.

The stage didn't offer the opportunity for private conversation, but it did give more chance for reflection than they'd known in the Gardiner's busy home. Elizabeth used some of that time for her own tumultuous thoughts and some for the study of Jane. Though her sister's emotions were hidden behind her usual appearance of serenity,

Elizabeth was sure there was still an underlying sadness clinging to Jane. Her sister, it seemed, had not yet gotten over Mr. Bingley and his ill use.

When they disembarked in the town where the Bennets' carriage was supposed to meet them, Elizabeth was surprised to find it wasn't there. She'd written their father they would return today and received confirmation they would be met. It was only about six miles to Longbourn, sticking to the road, but they couldn't make the trip with their luggage.

"Do you think they have forgotten us?" she asked, turning to Jane.

"I daresay they're simply late. Let us wait a while and I am sure the carriage will arrive soon."

The three women went to the inn to wait. Maria Lucas was worried the carriage had lost a wheel. Jane calmed her fears and kindly engaged her in a discussion of what they would order at the inn. When the meal was eaten without the arrival of the carriage, Elizabeth inquired about hiring some conveyance to bring them home.

She soon located an inexpensive vehicle for hire. It was the only conveyance available within their means, but it didn't have enough room for all of them and their possessions. Not wanting to wait for another opportunity, she hired it regardless, telling the driver only Jane and Maria would need to ride.

Since Maria was becoming agitated at the wait, and since Lucas Lodge was no further than Longbourn, Elizabeth and Jane quickly decided to take Maria home first.

"I'll walk," Elizabeth said. "I've been inactive too long, and I'll enjoy it."

"Walk swiftly, then, or Lady Lucas will send out a carriage to find you," Jane said. She gave Elizabeth a smile and allowed the driver to hand her up.

It was a beautiful day for walking, made all the more delightful by the familiar scenery. When Elizabeth got close to Longbourn, she cut across a field, hungry for a glimpse of home after nearly two months' absence. She hurried up the final hill, knowing the house would be visible when she reached the crest. A smile on her face, she scanned the countryside before her.

Her searching gaze met with a smoldering ruin.

She broke into a run, her heart thrashing violently in her chest. When she got close, it was even worse than she'd thought. There was nothing left but the hearths. Wildly, she looked about, an anguished cry bubbling from her lips.

Where was everyone? Where was Jane? What had happened?

"Miss Bennet," a voice called.

Elizabeth turned to see a woman walking toward her, coming from the direction of one of the tenant cottages, a baby on her hip.

"Mrs. Smith," Elizabeth cried. With a shudder, she turned from the still smoking ruins and ran toward the woman. "What has happened?"

"There was a fire," Mrs. Smith said, unnecessarily. She shook her head, the movement slow and drenched in sorrow.

"Where is my family?"

"Dead."

"All of them?" Elizabeth asked in horror.

"Aye." Mrs. Smith drew in a long breath. She rocked the baby, though it didn't fuss, only watched Elizabeth with wide eyes. "Your parents are dead, and your younger sisters with them."

"Dead?" Elizabeth repeated. She took a step backward, dizziness assailing her.

"I'm sorry, miss."

Still looking at Elizabeth with wide eyes, the baby started to cry.

It was in a dazed blur Elizabeth, through the kindness of neighbors, eventually found herself at the Phillips. She walked up the steps and stood, unable to knock. Her mind filled with the image of her burned home. With such a fire and Mrs. Smith's word for it, she knew her family must be gone. Still, it seemed almost as if, were she not to enter and hear it from the respected figure of her uncle, it may not really be true.

The door opened, revealing the very man of her thoughts. "Elizabeth," Uncle Phillips said. "I was on my way to look for you. Jane is inside."

Elizabeth stared at him. She couldn't think of anything to say.

"Come in, dear," he said, stepping back and gesturing her into the hall.

Her movements stiff, Elizabeth stepped inside.

"You've heard, I take it?" her uncle asked in a quiet voice.

Elizabeth nodded. Tears built up in her eyes and she blinked, sending them streaming down her cheeks. "I saw the house," she said. Rather, those were the words she meant to say, but all that emerged were garbled sobs.

Her uncle put his arms about her, patting her on the back. Elizabeth gave in to her sorrow, weeping on his shoulder. It took her long moments to collect herself enough to relinquish her hold on him and allow him to lead her to Jane. Her only relief was that Jane had received the news at Lucas Lodge, not by the burnt-out shell that was once Longbourn.

***

The funerals took place that Saturday, the Gardiners

arriving the day before. After their parents and sisters were laid to rest, Elizabeth and Jane sat down with their aunts and uncles in the Phillips parlor. Elizabeth knew they were there to discuss her and Jane's futures. She tried to muster the necessary interest, but her grief was too fresh for her to convince herself to care.

The only thing to penetrate the sorrow weighing on her was how wan Jane looked. Gentle soul that she was, Jane seemed to be even more distraught than Elizabeth. Elizabeth reached out and took her sister's hand. Squaring her shoulders, she resolved to attempt something better approaching normality, for Jane's sake.

Silence settled over the room, punctuated by the rustle of people fidgeting. Everyone looked about, avoiding each other's eyes. It was obvious no one knew where to begin.

"How are the servants?" Mr. Gardiner said, his tone gruff.

"Three of them have already found new employment," Mr. Phillips said. "The fourth, a maid, had already planned to marry a local farmer."

Mr. Gardiner nodded. Elizabeth realized she recalled hearing one of the maids was to wed. Mrs. Smith had named the servants who survived as well as those who hadn't. Elizabeth briefly regretted so little of her grief was for the servants who died. Her family's deaths were so overwhelming that the other deaths seemed inappropriately trivial. She resolved to include them in her prayers.

"As to the property, it is not our concern," Mr. Phillips said. "Since the estate was entailed, the heir will decide what to do about it."

Mrs. Gardiner leaned forward, clasping her hands before her. "Jane and Elizabeth should return with us to London. We have a room they can share."

"You have four children of your own to think of," Mrs.

Phillips said, her tone sharp. "Consider the expense of two more mouths."

"The interest on the five thousand pounds their mother had should easily cover their expenses and give them an allowance."

Elizabeth squeezed Jane's hand, seeing tears form in her eyes at the mention of their mother.

Mr. Phillips cleared his throat. "There's something you should know about that money."

"If it isn't there, we will still take them in," Mr. Gardiner said. "We may have to cut a few corners, but we know our responsibility." He turned to look at Elizabeth and Jane. "And it will be our pleasure to have you."

Aunt Gardiner added a smiling nod to their uncle's words. "Of course, we will, and it truly would."

"No, we will take them in," Mrs. Phillips said. "Mr. Phillips and I have already decided."

"There are many advantages to living in London," Mrs. Gardiner said. "Jane and Elizabeth will flourish there."

Elizabeth wasn't certain that was true. She looked to Jane, but her sister's face was too wreathed in sorrow for Elizabeth to read her feelings on where they might live. She wished she'd thought to speak with Jane on the subject before now. Elizabeth might argue a side for them, but only if she knew what would better alleviate Jane's sorrow.

"They've had enough disruption in their lives. They should be surrounded by people they know," Mrs. Phillips countered.

"It would not be a disruption for Jane. She's spent months with us," Mrs. Gardiner said. "It will be good for them to get away from Hertfordshire and the sad memories here."

"If I may intervene," Mr. Phillips said. "I think what my wife is trying to express is your household will inevitably be centered around your young family. We will center ours around our nieces. We've never been blessed with children. I have no other living relatives. I've watched them grow up since they were infants, seeing them weekly. They are the daughters we never had. Please don't deprive us of them."

"We have to do what is best for them, not for us," Mrs. Gardiner said, looking more stubborn than Elizabeth had ever seen her.

"I can't argue with that, but I can disagree with what is best for them," Mr. Phillips countered.

The argument continued. Although the words remained polite, the voices were becoming strained. Elizabeth watched Jane carefully, gauging her level of distress. When it became too great, she decided she must try, at least, to make something happy of their circumstance. She leaned toward her sister, whispering, "At least they all want us. It would be awful if they were each arguing we should live with the other."

Jane managed a trembling smile, but tears stood out in her eyes. Elizabeth knew she must do something to stop the argument. Jane was becoming too upset and no progress toward a solution seemed to be forthcoming.

Were it up to Elizabeth alone, she would have chosen her London relatives, whom she preferred, though her Meryton ones had more space. Not knowing Jane's mind, though, and wanting to spare everyone's feelings, Elizabeth felt the solution was obvious. "We could spend half a year with each of you."

Mr. Gardiner and Mr. Phillips eyed each other. They looked to their wives. Mrs. Gardiner gave a miniscule nod. Mrs. Phillips looked rebellious but shrugged.

"I think that should be adjusted as needed," Mrs. Gardiner said. "It is too early to be thinking about suitors, but if someone is courting one of them, they should not be removed prematurely if it looks like a good connection."

"Yes," said Mrs. Phillips. She brightened. "Living in two locations will give them a better chance of meeting someone eligible. We all want that." She leaned across the table and patted Jane on the hand.

Elizabeth shook her head. She had no interest in courtship from any man. Her grief was still too new for her to struggle out from beneath the weight of it. There was no way she'd be able to manage the sort of amiability one should present to a suitor.

"Now, you were saying something about the money?" Mr. Gardiner asked Mr. Phillips, leaning back in his chair.

"Yes. Early on in their marriage, Mr. Bennet became concerned Mrs. Bennet was too extravagant. He didn't want to fight with her over money, but he was worried about it. He had to disclose his income, because of tithing, but his expenses, well, you know how expensive it is to run a farm." He looked about the table. "Well, no matter the details. The upshot is, he managed to put away around ten percent of his income almost every year without Mrs. Bennet knowing it."

Elizabeth raised her eyebrows. For a moment, surprise chased away grief. She'd no idea her father had such foresight, or was so cunning, or so economical.

"Mr. Phillips was doing the same with me," Mrs. Phillips said. The smile she gave her husband was indulgent. "I only found out about it two years ago."

"Two hundred pounds for more than twenty years," said Mr. Gardiner. "That comes to more than four thousand pounds."

"You forgot interest. It's closer to six thousand. Jane and Elizabeth will each have a bit more than five thousand pounds. Considering their situation, after their expenses and allowances are taken out, I believe the remainder of the money should be reinvested."

Elizabeth realized she was still staring at her Uncle Phillips and looked down. It was a great relief to know they were loved, and they wouldn't be a burden on those who cared for them. More than that, the money they would each have gave them a level of independence Elizabeth had never dared to hope for. She suppressed a sigh. The only bad thing was, without money to worry over, her mind had only the death of her parents and sisters to dwell on.

CHAPTER TWO

Darcy listened to his sister, Georgiana, play the pianoforte with mixed feelings. She played beautifully and he enjoyed the music, but he suspected she played simply to avoid speaking with his guests. He'd already determined not to bring her out this coming season. She was still too shy. That her shyness extended to the Bingleys and the Hursts, whom she knew very well, served to emphasize the wisdom of Darcy's decision. How would Georgiana be able to cope with the numerous people she would have to meet during the season if she couldn't bring herself to interact with frequent companions?

On the score of Miss Bingley, Darcy concurred with his sister. Miss Bingley wasn't a comfortable guest. Her obvious attempts to attract him were very wearing. If Bingley weren't the most amiable of gentlemen, Darcy wouldn't routinely place himself within the same sphere as Bingley's sister.

Miss Bingley hadn't always been as trying. In truth, he hadn't noticed her behavior very much in the past. Her flattery had mirrored his typical lot and her pomposity had seemed reasonable. The change wasn't in Miss Bingley's behavior toward or around him, but more in himself.

Elizabeth Bennet had fully revealed her feelings for Darcy, and they had not been what he hoped, or even expected. Instead of admiring him as was his general due, especially from women in want of a husband, she'd criticized him. She'd gone so far as to accuse him of having a selfish disdain of the feelings of others. She'd labeled him a snob and elitist of the worst sort.

Looking about at the company he kept, Darcy was forced to consider the merit of her words. Miss Bingley, who sat watching Georgiana with obviously feigned delight, was trying to attract him and did everything she could to divide the world into people who were worth associating with and people who weren't. She looked down on the vast majority of people, as few fit her restricted criteria.

Her sister, Mrs. Hurst, wasn't quite as much of a sycophant as Miss Bingley, but she held just as many people in low esteem. That stood as proof of her snootiness, as she obviously valued social standing more than personal merit. Mrs. Hurst's husband was of unquestionably good lineage, but held only a modest estate, with an income of about half of what Mr. Bennet had. Mr. Hurst lived for his meals, naps, and cards.

Darcy had always tolerated Miss Bingley and the Hursts because of his friendship with Bingley and because they were the people he was expected to associate with. They were of the correct social class, age and lineages, though there was the shadow of trade in the Bingleys' past. Were those criteria truly the best way to establish with whom to fill one's days?

Darcy looked about the room again. Miss Bingley, seeing his gaze on her, stifled a yawn and gave him a fawning smile. Mrs. Hurst was playing with her bracelets, not even pretending to enjoy Georgiana's performance. Mr. Hurst was asleep on the sofa.

Maybe Georgiana had a point. Maybe Darcy should find a way to avoid talking to most of his guests. The more he considered his reasons for the company he kept, the less substantial they seemed. Instead, why not surround himself with people whose company he actually cared for, regardless of their station?

Darcy glanced over his shoulder at Bingley, wondering if he would be up for a game of billiards. Bingley was seated at a desk, going through the post. At least he wasn't pretending to pay attention, though he was sure to get an earful from his sisters later for not making the effort. Darcy would be daft not to realize they had ideas about Bingley wedding Georgiana. In spite of Bingley's imperfect lineage, Darcy would have welcomed the match, were there any sign of romantic affection between them. Even before Elizabeth's criticism of him had awakened him to some of his less savory characteristics, Darcy knew it would be better for his sister to have a man as good hearted and financially sound as Bingley than one with a title.

"Oh, no," Bingley exclaimed.

"What is the matter?" Darcy asked, turning more fully around in his seat.

Georgiana's fingers stilled on the keys.

"Sir William Lucas wrote me. Longbourn has burned down. The family died."

Darcy's heart froze in his chest. Elizabeth, dead?

"Poor Miss Bennet," Miss Bingley said. "She was very lovely."

"She wasn't home," Bingley said, his eyes fixed on the words he was reading.

The relief in Bingley's voice spoke volumes, his expression shifting from horrified to merely troubled. Darcy was peripherally aware of Bingley's sisters exchanging looks. He watched Bingley read on, too shocked by the loss of Elizabeth to speak.

"Neither was her sister Elizabeth," Bingley said.

Logically, Darcy knew it had been mere seconds between revelations, but an eternity of time drew to a close at Bingley's words. Darcy found himself able to breathe again, his heart shuddering back to life. He realized there was pain in his hands and looked down, finding them tightly fisted. Slowly, he uncurled his fingers.

"The Miss Elizabeth Bennet you wrote to me of?" Georgiana asked from her seat at the piano.

Glancing at his sister, Darcy also took in Miss Bingley's narrowed eyes and the flash of loathing there. "Yes, that Miss Elizabeth." Darcy turned back to Bingley. "You mean to say Mr. and Mrs. Bennet are gone, along with the home and three younger sisters?"

"Yes. Miss Bennet and Miss Elizabeth were safely away. Sir William says they'd been in London, Miss Bennet for some time." Bingley glanced at Miss Bingley. "I'm surprised she didn't call on you when she was in London."

"She did," Mr. Hurst said, surprising Darcy, who hadn't realized he was awake. "Sometime in January, I think. Your sisters returned the call a month later."

Everyone looked at him.

Bingley surged to his feet, swiveling to face Miss Bingley. "Why didn't you tell me?"

"Because I thought it wouldn't be good for you to see her," Miss Bingley said. "Louisa and I thought you were too likely to fall under her spell again."

"What else does the letter say?" Darcy asked, wanting to avoid further discussion of Miss Bennet's visit to London. He'd known she was there and had gone along with Miss Bingley's decision not to inform Bingley.

Bingley looked down. "Miss Bennet and Miss Elizabeth will be spending their summers in Meryton with the Phillips and their winters in London with the Gardiners."

"Transferred from household to household," Miss Bingley said. "That's what happens to poor, unwanted relatives, and they are going between a country attorney and a man in trade."

Bingley lifted an angry visage. "The behavior of their relatives does not make them less worthy or less kind."

"True," Darcy said, eliciting several startled looks.

Bingley sat abruptly, reaching for a clean page. "I must write her and offer my condolences."

No one asked who Bingley meant by *her*.

"You can't write her," Miss Bingley cried.

Bingley paused in the act of preparing writing supplies. He frowned, turning to Darcy.

"You really can't," Darcy said. "You can write Mr. and Mrs. Phillips and offer them your condolences."

"Yes. That's what you should do," Miss Bingley said. She cast Darcy a smile.

Bingley was still frowning, a deep line marking his brow. He shook his head. "I'm going to do more than that. I'm going there." He stood once more.

"Charles, no," Mrs. Hurst exclaimed, but Bingley left the room.

Darcy was torn between the foolishness of Bingley returning to Hertfordshire and a longing to accompany him. Surely, Bingley knew to return now would be tantamount to a proposal to Miss Bennet? Or would it be? He leased a house there and should be able to come and go as he pleased. There would be speculation, but that should not matter. Did Bingley care about that? Considering the look of terror on Bingley's face when he took in the first words of the letter, maybe he didn't mind the speculation that he might marry Miss Bennet, because he planned to do so.

Leaving the piano, Georgiana came over to sit beside Darcy.

"Mr. Hurst, do something," Mrs. Hurst cried.

"I am doing something." Mr. Hurst settled back onto the sofa. "I'm taking a nap."

"Louisa, we can't permit him to go," Miss Bingley said.

"You know how he is. It was all we could do to keep him from proposing to that low woman before. Imagine now, when she's in distress? There will be no stopping him."

Georgiana touched Darcy's sleeve. "Since this is the same Miss Elizabeth you wrote me about last autumn, perhaps you should go with Mr. Bingley," she said in a soft voice. "It must have been awful for her to lose her family and home."

"That's a good idea," he said, standing.

"What?" Miss Bingley said. "You too, Mr. Darcy? What is this draw Hertfordshire has?"

Darcy could tell by the venomous undertones in her voice she suspected what the allure of Hertfordshire was, and did not condone it. He bowed to the room. "I beg your leave."

"Mr. Darcy, at least assure us that you go there to prevent Charles from doing anything foolish," Mrs. Hurst said.

"I can assure you of that, madam." There was no reason to elaborate on the fact he was growing more and more certain the only foolish thing Bingley could do would be not to propose to Miss Bennet. "Georgiana," he added with another bow, returning his sister's smiled.

As he strode from the room, Darcy assured himself that him being there wouldn't be in any way a public declaration of affection. People would assume he was there to support Bingley, as he would, in whatever choice Bingley made. Unless Elizabeth had revealed his proposal, something he did not think she would do, no one had reason to suspect his true motives were much more convoluted.

He must assure himself Elizabeth was being well provided for and, at the same time, attempt to understand his inability to put her from his thoughts, in spite of her adamant and thorough rejection. Maybe seeing her again would rid him of the demon that was his affection for her.

Or maybe seeing him again, changed as he was by her words, would soften her regard. He preferred that scenario. Smiling, Darcy strode through Pemberley, making ready to travel.

CHAPTER THREE

It took Elizabeth little time to realize no amount of financial hardship would have distracted from the harsh reality of her family's death. Everything they did seemed to center around death. They made black gowns. They endured seemingly endless condolence calls and received piles of well-intentioned letters.

Elizabeth answered the letters as politely as she could. She took on the bulk of that task as Jane kept crying and smearing the ink. Jane did her best with the callers, sitting beside Elizabeth in bereaved silence while uncomfortable people spoke platitudes. Most people were very kind to them, which did help to buoy Elizabeth's spirits. Many more came than she would have expected, like Colonel Forster, commander of the local militia, who was very polite and thoughtful.

Another unexpected, and to Elizabeth's mind unwanted, caller was Lieutenant Wickham. He entered with a too-low bow and a charming smile. Elizabeth wondered how she could ever have considered his smug and ingratiating countenance pleasing.

"What lovely ladies," he said. "I didn't know black could make someone so attractive."

He included her Aunt Phillips in his sweeping glance, but his gaze came to rest on Jane, where it lingered overlong. Elizabeth found that odd, as he'd never paid Jane much attention before. Jane met his regard with a tentative smile.

In that moment, Elizabeth wished she'd made the time to enlighten Jane on the truth of Mr. Wickham's character while they'd been in London with the Gardiners. Not that there hadn't been time since returning, but her mind had been too occupied with the loss of their family to think about Mr. Wickham and Mr. Darcy.

"I've come to add my deepest sympathies to the well wishes I'm sure you've already garnered," Mr. Wickham said. "To lose your family, and you both still so young, is a tragedy indeed."

"Thank you," Jane murmured.

"I realize you, in particular, Miss Bennet, are of a very sensitive nature," he continued. "I know this time must be very trying for you indeed."

Jane looked to Elizabeth, her brow creased, before turning back to Mr. Wickham. "Elizabeth and I are both quite distraught."

"Yes, but your sister must admit you are the more sensitive. You may think I hadn't noticed, but how could I not?"

Jane looked to her again.

Elizabeth frowned. "It is true, Mr. Wickham. Jane's sensitive nature is legendary, which is why we must not distress her by speaking of it, or by allowing any visitors to stay over long."

"I agree with you on the first count, Miss Elizabeth." Mr. Wickham didn't look at her, but kept his smile aimed at Jane. "I beg your pardon for disagreeing on the second, however. I think the distraction of company is what Miss Bennet wants. Distraction and, dare I suggest, a walk?"

"Certainly," Jane said the same time as Elizabeth said, "No, thank you," in overly strident tones.

Jane turned a sad smile on Elizabeth. "I would like to get out, but I don't wish to inconvenience you, Lizzy. I'm sure

Mr. Wickham will keep me respectful company."

Elizabeth wished more than ever she'd told Jane Mr. Wickham was no longer in her favor. "If you wish to walk, I shall accompany you."

"No, I wouldn't think of imposing on you," Jane said. "I'd rather not go out than do so."

"Surely you would not deprive your sister of some respite from her grief?" Mr. Wickham said.

"No, I would not," Elizabeth replied, trying not to glare at him. She no longer trusted him as she might once have. "Do go on, Jane. I'm content to remain here. Stay on the streets, though, won't you. We don't have a maid to send along."

She gave them both a smile, settling back in her seat. She did want Jane to get out. It had been weeks since their return. There was no reason her sister should sit there mourning at all moments of the day. If allowing Jane to walk with Mr. Wickham was what it took to see her happy, then Elizabeth would allow it, but she wouldn't let Jane go unchaperoned. She would make a reason to go after them.

"Miss Elizabeth, Mrs. Phillips," Mr. Wickham said, bowing.

Jane stood and he offered his arm, increasing Elizabeth's unease. She kept her smile in place until they left the room.

"Oh, what a handsome young man Mr. Wickham is," Mrs. Phillips said. "Only, I thought he was a friend of yours, Elizabeth. Why should he ask Jane to walk?"

"You know, Aunt Phillips, I should like to find out," Elizabeth said, standing. "I think I shall join them after all. It may be I can tease his reasons from him."

"I daresay teasing is at the heart of it, Elizabeth. You didn't show yourself pleased enough to see him, as you ought to have, so he is teasing you by paying attention to Jane. Don't let that go on too long, dear, or he'll take a liking to her. There's no man could resist taking a liking to our Jane, given half a chance."

"I'm sure you're right," Elizabeth said. Hurrying from the room, she fetched her bonnet and went outside. She could see Jane farther down the street, on Mr. Wickham's arm. Pressing her lips into a firm line, Elizabeth strode after them.

She didn't join them, but rather trailed behind. She truly didn't wish to ruin any slight enjoyment Jane could contrive from the day. She simply couldn't bring herself to trust Mr. Wickham, though. There was something unsettling in the way he was lavishing attention on Jane.

The day was warm enough, but it was windy and fluffy clouds sailed through the sky high above. Elizabeth followed them down the street and up the lane, worried when it appeared they were leaving town. Once free of Meryton, they paused beside a little used path. Elizabeth could see Jane shake her head, dropping his arm. Mr. Wickham leaned close, speaking animatedly. Jane hesitated a moment, then nodded. He offered his arm again and Jane hesitantly took it.

As they started up the path, Elizabeth lengthened her strides, closing the distance between them and keeping Jane in sight. She was doubly concerned now. There was no reason for Mr. Wickham to persuade Jane to go meandering through such a relatively uninhabited area. Not one Elizabeth would approve of, leastwise.

She drew closer but still didn't join them. In the time it took her to shorten the distance, restraint had somewhat reasserted itself. Jane was perfectly intelligent and very proper. If she'd agreed with whatever Mr. Wickham had said to her, it was likely acceptable. There was no reason for Elizabeth to barge in on their walk and make a hash of things.

A cottage drew into view, the reason for the path, though Elizabeth knew it had been abandoned the past summer. It stood atop a hill on a bit of cleared land and Elizabeth hung back farther. She didn't want them to turn to appreciate the view, likely why they'd come, and spot her.

Elizabeth moved behind some tall bushes, peeking out from the obscuring brush. She was feeling more and more like the worst sort of voyeur and a terrible sister. She pursed her lips, wondering if she should return to the Phillips. After all, Jane and Mr. Wickham must return the way they'd come, and what explanation would she have when they spotted her ahead of them on the way back?

As they crested the hill, Mr. Wickham dropped to the ground. Elizabeth went still in surprise, wondering what had befallen him. Jane came to her knees beside him. Elizabeth could see them speaking animatedly and hear their worried tones, but she couldn't make out the words. Jane stood. With what seemed like effort on both parts, Jane helped Mr. Wickham to his feet. He pointed toward the cottage. Jane ducked under his arm, helping him toward it.

Worried for both Jane and Mr. Wickham, Elizabeth untangled her skirts from the brush she hid in. Returning to the trail, she hurried up the remaining distance to the cottage. Reaching it, she was surprised to find the door closed. Tentatively, she pushed against it, but it didn't budge, appearing to be bolted.

Suddenly weary again, Elizabeth didn't knock. She backed away, looking about the clearing to no avail. With hurried steps, she circled the cottage, stopping when she found a window. It was shuttered, but several of the slats were missing. Ducking slightly, she peered in.

The cottage was filled with more light than she would have expected, mainly coming from a hole in the roof. Still, it took Elizabeth a moment to sort out their forms in the gloomy interior. When she did, she found Mr. Wickham with his back to the door. Jane stood across the room from him. Though in profile, Elizabeth could see the startled look on her face.

"…the door?" Jane was saying.

"So we may go undisturbed, my love," Mr. Wickham said.

Elizabeth gasped, smothering the sound with her hand.

"Your… I beg your pardon?" Jane said.

"Miss Bennet, you must allow me to tell you how ardently I admire and love you."

"What?"

"I had to get you alone." Mr. Wickham walked toward her. "The regiment will be leaving in a few days. I missed you all winter. I thought my case was hopeless, because you were taken in by Mr. Bingley."

"Taken in?" Jane stared at him, obviously dumfounded.

"Yes. He never cared for you as I do. Why would he leave you if he truly loved you? I, however, have remained."

"He…he may come back. He said he would come back."

Mr. Wickham was quite near Jane now. Elizabeth wanted to tell her to run, but where would Jane run to? Jane stared at him as he moved closer and closer. Reaching out, he grabbed for her.

Jane tried to duck away, but he was quicker. He pulled her to him, pressing his lips to hers. She thrashed, wrenching her head away and flailing at him ineffectually. Elizabeth cried out, yanking on the shutters.

Mr. Wickham stopped moving, looking about. Elizabeth went still. He peered toward the window.

Jane pulled free. "Mr. Wickham. What are you doing? This is not appropriate." She angled around him, moving toward the door.

Mr. Wickham turned back to Jane. "You are

compromised. You have no choice but to marry me. You don't know how happy—"

"She certainly is not," Elizabeth cried through the window.

Mr. Wickham whirled, looking startled. Behind him, Jane crept toward the door.

"I've been here all along," Elizabeth said, striving to make enough commotion so Mr. Wickham wouldn't realize Jane was escaping his grasp. "I saw everything. You should be ashamed of yourself, Mr. Wickham."

"She has to marry me. After word of this gets out, no one else will have her," Mr. Wickham said.

"She's better off never marrying than wedding you," Elizabeth said.

Jane reached the door. Mr. Wickham turned as she pulled the latch open, but she flung the door wide and rushed out. Abandoning her post at the window, Elizabeth ran back around the house. She found Mr. Wickham on his knees before Jane, holding one of her hands, though she was obviously trying to pull away.

"Jane," he said.

"She is not Jane to you," Elizabeth snapped, hurrying to Jane's side.

"Miss Bennet," Mr. Wickham continued, shooting Elizabeth a scowl. "You must know how beautiful you are and how you can drive a man to distraction. That is what happened just now, but I will do right by you. I love you. Marry me."

Jane wrenched her hand away.

Elizabeth caught a glimpse of how red it was before Jane cradled it against her chest.

Jane drew her shoulders back, raising her chin. "I would rather remain alone than be coerced into marrying you."

"You may have to test that. You know I'm right. No one

else will take you now."

Jane glared at him.

Mr. Wickham stood. He shrugged, dusting off his uniform. "Have it your way. Once you realize I've spoken the truth, you'll come begging me to take you."

Elizabeth and Jane trained matching looks of disdain on him. He gave them a jaunty smile before turning and walking away. Just before he disappeared into the woods, he looked back and waved.

Long moments passed while they waited, making sure he was gone. Elizabeth heard a ragged inhalation and looked over to see Jane on the verge of tears. Turning, she took Jane into her arms. Elizabeth made no attempt to stop her from crying, even though Jane sobbed the entire walk back to Meryton. Anyone seeing them would attribute Jane's tears to understandable grief.

CHAPTER FOUR

Darcy and Bingley called upon Mr. Phillips the same day they arrived in Hertfordshire. They were shown into a small parlor. Looking about, Darcy could see the contents of the room were not new, but were well cared for and in decent, though outdated, taste. All and all, it was a nicer room than he would have credited the Phillips and rather pleasant.

It would have been made exceedingly pleasant had it contained Elizabeth and Miss Bennet, but they were absent. Darcy settled into a chair, aware it wouldn't be in good form to ask about their whereabouts. Bingley, his gaze searching the room in an obvious manner, slowly sat as well.

"Mr. Darcy, Mr. Bingley," Mr. Phillips said. "This is a pleasant surprise, though quite unexpected. Have you decided to return to Netherfield Park, Mr. Bingley?"

"I should like to." Bingley leaned forward in his chair. "That is, I mean to, depending…Rather, we shall see." He looked to Darcy for help.

"We've come to express our condolences," Darcy supplied.

"All this way? That is exceedingly generous of you." Mr. Phillips studied them for a moment. "I am remiss in not offering you refreshments."

"That isn't necessary," Darcy said.

"I should have thought to offer immediately, of course. I do tend to forget these things when my wife isn't about to remind me. Mrs. Phillips is currently at Lucas Lodge." He smiled slightly. "Jane and Elizabeth have taken a walk.

They've been gone some time. Are you sure you wouldn't care for something?"

Bingley gave him a pleading look. Darcy was tempted to take Mr. Phillips up on his offer to allow them to remain until Elizabeth and Miss Bennet returned. After this call, their condolences having been offered, they would have no ready excuse to return.

"Uncle," Elizabeth said, bursting into the room.

Darcy turned to her, astounded anew by the uncommon loveliness of her face. How he couldn't have noticed it on their initial meeting, he didn't know. She was especially lovely in that moment, her eyes flashing and face flushed.

"Pardon me," Elizabeth said, looking about the room. Her eyes met his questioningly. "I did not realize we had guests."

"Miss Elizabeth," Darcy said, standing to bow.

Mr. Phillips and Bingley stood as well, offering their greetings.

"Mr. Darcy." Elizabeth dropped a curtsy.

"Miss Bennet," Bingley said bowing a second time.

Darcy could see Bingley was looking past Elizabeth. For the first time, he realized her sister hovered behind her. Miss Bennet was rapidly wiping her eyes and cheeks. He gathered she'd been crying. When he turned back to Elizabeth, Darcy realized anger flashed in her eyes. Could she be that displeased to see him? Or was Bingley the focus of her ire? She'd made no secret of thinking he'd broken her sister's heart.

"Uncle," Elizabeth reiterated. She reached back, taking Miss Bennet's arm and tugging her into the room.

Darcy frowned. Something was not right in the image of the two young ladies before him. Miss Bennet seemed almost afraid, and now that Elizabeth was casting off her surprise at seeing them, her anger was a palpable thing.

Darcy couldn't bring himself to think anyone in the room was deserving of that much animosity, even him.

"What's wrong, my dear?" Mr. Phillips came forward to take Miss Bennet's hands.

"What is wrong is that Mr. Wickham attempted to compromise Jane." Elizabeth's voice was fierce. She wrapped an arm about Miss Bennet's shoulder.

"He did what?" Bingley exclaimed. He looked about as if seeking the man.

"He tricked her into taking an unused path," Elizabeth said.

"He told me Lydia had spoken to him of a place she loved to go, where she'd secreted some small sentimental objects she adored. He said he wanted to help me find them so we could have something to remember her by," Miss Bennet said, her voice breaking as tears overwhelmed her once more.

"He lured Jane into the Evans' abandoned cottage and locked the door," Elizabeth said. "Not trusting him, I was following them. When the door wouldn't open, I went round to a window. He grabbed her and forced his attentions on her."

"He did what?" Bingley repeated, looking stunned.

"He only kissed me," Miss Bennet said, her face turning red. "It was awful."

"He kissed you and demanded you marry him." Elizabeth was clearly livid.

Darcy reflected Wickham was fortunate Miss Elizabeth wasn't a man. Elsewise, Wickham would be forced to meet her at dawn. Darcy was sorely tempted to call his onetime playmate out himself. Coercing women was a new low for Wickham.

"He's a kidnapper," Bingley said.

"I doubt a court would see it that way," Mr. Phillips said,

shaking his head.

"I'll challenge him to a duel," Bingley said.

Darcy could see his friend's astonishment was shifting into anger. "If you are trying to preserve Miss Bennet's reputation, that won't help." Darcy watched Bingley comprehend the situation. A duel fought over a woman, especially by a man who was not a relative, would seriously damage her reputation.

"Dueling is illegal," Mr. Phillips said with a sigh. "Yes, I've been wishing I were twenty years younger and was adept with both sword and pistol for the last few minutes, but it would accomplish nothing."

"If I may be so insensitive as to ask, why does Mr. Wickham want to marry Miss Bennet?" Darcy asked. "I thought Mr. Bennet had little to leave and am familiar with what Wickham seeks in a spouse."

"There is a rumor going around that the Miss Bennets are heiresses."

Something about the closed look on Mr. Phillips' face and his tone made Darcy wonder how much truth there was to the rumor. Could Mr. Bennet have been a better businessman than Darcy surmised?

"Mr. Wickham nearly succeeded in marrying an heiress, Miss Mary King, a month ago," Mr. Phillips continued. "Her uncle took her away."

"He said he's always loved me," Miss Bennet said. "He claimed he never said anything before because he knew he couldn't compete wi--" She broke off, her tear-filled eyes going to Bingley.

"I don't find it a stretch to believe a man could be driven to distraction by Miss Bennet's beauty," Bingley said.

Darcy raised his eyebrows. A glance showed him similar expressions on Elizabeth's and Mr. Phillips' faces. Bingley and Miss Bennet looked at each other, seemingly unaware of anyone else.

Elizabeth turned to Darcy. "As little as I think of Mr. Wickham's character, this seems a rash action even for him."

"Mr. Wickham likely has debts," Darcy said.

"He does," Mr. Phillips said. When they turned to him, he shrugged. "An attorney hears things others don't. I've told two of my clients they should take action against him before his unit leaves or lose their money. Neither want to do so, because he is popular. Now, I wonder if I should stop pressing them. If he faced debtors' prison and knew the source, the first thing he would do would be to malign Jane. Though I admit, it would give me satisfaction to see the man locked away, and if he didn't learn the source, it may be the best protection for her."

Darcy frowned. He wouldn't mind seeing Wickham locked away either, but he doubted it would come to that. Instead, Wickham would attempt to blackmail Darcy into paying his debts again by threatening to expose Georgiana's near elopement with him. Darcy caught Elizabeth's eyes on him and wondered if her thoughts traversed a similar path.

"Locked away?" Miss Bennet repeated. She'd dried her tears again and looked steadier by far than when she and Elizabeth had arrived. "I shouldn't wish to be responsible for anyone going to prison. I wouldn't be able to live with knowing I'd caused anyone such suffering, even Mr. Wickham."

"But he attempted to force you into marriage." Bingley's tone evidenced anger once more. "He deserves prison or worse."

"I still don't want it to be done over me."

"He wouldn't go to debtors' prison because of you, dear," Mr. Phillips said. "He would go because of his debts. It is, after all, where he belongs by dint of his behavior. We must do something to prevent him from slandering your reputation and ruining your prospects."

Taking in the way Bingley looked at Miss Bennet, Darcy didn't think she needed to fear for her marriage prospects. Miss Bennet didn't know that, however. She turned a pleading look on her sister.

"Though we cannot control the actions of everyone in the community, I ask that none of you consider putting Mr. Wickham in debtor's prison," Elizabeth said in a firm tone. "I have no wish for my sister to allot any of her kind spirit to worrying over Mr. Wickham. Causing Jane more misery will not alleviate the upset he's produced and will instead only place more unhappiness on her shoulders."

Miss Bennet cast Elizabeth a grateful smile.

Darcy gave a nod of his head to indicate his understanding. "Would you mind if we threaten Mr. Wickham with debtors' prison?" Darcy thought Miss Bennet too tender hearted, but she wouldn't be a fitting match for Bingley if she weren't. As he could observe how much Bingley cared for her, he must be pleased by her gentle nature instead of regretting it.

"What do you have in mind?" Elizabeth asked.

"Can anyone speculate on the next time Mr. Wickham will be in public?" Darcy asked.

"Tonight, at Lucas Lodge," Mr. Phillips said. "Sir William is throwing a party for the officers. We are invited, but I'd thought not to attend, considering."

"I should like to attend," Bingley said. "I have a thing or two to say to Mr. Wickham. But I don't believe we were invited."

"No one knows you are in town," Elizabeth said. "I am sure Sir William would never turn you away, however."

Darcy nodded, acknowledging the likely truth of her statement. "Knowing Wickham as I do, I think I can say with surety he will attend the event. He will not miss a chance to be charming and partake of food and drink provided by another, and he will not fear meeting either of you because you are still in mourning. I propose we all attend Sir William's event. I have a plan which I think shall satisfy everyone, but it requires us all to participate."

"Then let us hear it," Mr. Phillips said.

All eyes turned to Darcy. He proceeded to elaborate on his plan. It pleased him to see how quickly both Elizabeth and her uncle registered understanding, and then satisfaction.

They spent nearly an hour discussing the details. In spite of the seriousness of the situation, Darcy thoroughly enjoyed himself. He knew his pleasure in the conversation stemmed in small part from contemplating Wickham's takedown and in great part from Elizabeth. Darcy hadn't enjoyed himself so much in quite some time. Not, in fact, since the last time he'd sparred with her.

Miss Bennet was timid at first, clearly still recovering from what had happened, and Darcy worried they wouldn't be able to carry off the plan. At Elizabeth's suggestion, they rehearsed their scenario several times, with her playing the part of Wickham. Darcy could tell each rendition increased Miss Bennet's confidence.

Mrs. Phillips returned, and Mr. Phillips explained everything to her, even giving her a role to play. She had trouble taking in both what had happened and the plot they'd hatched. After some time, however, Mr. Phillips' repeated explanations and a great deal of patience got Mrs. Phillips into the spirit of the thing.

At first, the need for the careful reconstruction of Mrs. Phillips' beliefs about Wickham tried Darcy's patience, though he was careful not to show it. As the conversation went on, he found himself contrasting Mr. Phillips' behavior toward his wife with Mr. Bennet's toward Mrs. Bennet. Darcy would never say anything to Elizabeth, but he thought Mr. Phillips was a better husband for an unintelligent woman than Mr. Bennet had been.

Darcy stood slightly to the side, watching Elizabeth take Miss Bennet and Mrs. Phillips through their final repetition of the plan. If Darcy had his way, he would never need to know what sort of husband he would make in similar circumstances. He would have Elizabeth, whose quick wit and clever tongue outshone even her lovely smile.

CHAPTER FIVE

Elizabeth followed Jane to their room to make ready for the evening. Now that she and Jane were alone, she was aware of sorrow threatening to overwhelm her once more. Almost angry at the emotion, she tamped it down as best she could. There was no way to lessen her heartbreak over losing her parents, sisters and home, but she knew she must be strong now for Jane. She fervently hoped Jane could be strong too. They had to get Mr. Wickham out of their lives and make sure he stayed out.

Mr. Darcy and Mr. Bingley had returned to Netherfield Park to make their preparations as well. As Elizabeth changed her gown and arranged her hair, she found contemplating Mr. Darcy's behavior a surprisingly effective distraction from her grief. She'd never seen him so relaxed and comfortable. He'd treated her Uncle Phillips with respect. No, Mr. Darcy had treated her uncle as an equal. On top of that, he hadn't shown the slightest bit of annoyance at either her aunt's slowness in learning her part or for Jane's timidity. It was a welcome change, for she couldn't have borne an afternoon with a haughty Mr. Darcy. Not with her nerves already stretched thin by mourning. Elizabeth thought kindness suited his eyes.

Later that evening as they trailed their aunt and uncle into Lucas Lodge, Elizabeth could see Jane's nervousness return. Jane stopped in the entry hall, for she was to wait above stairs in the youngest Lucas's room. He was a boy of about seven and adored Jane. Elizabeth knew he would ask her to read to him or play soldiers. She hoped it would keep Jane distracted until their aunt fetched her.

"It will all go just as we've planned," Elizabeth whispered.

"How can you be so certain?" Jane asked.

"Mr. Darcy knows Mr. Wickham quite well. They grew up together. Don't worry."

Jane managed a weak smile. "I feel awkward being here while we're still in deep mourning. People will think we didn't love Mama, Papa and our sisters enough." Jane was on the verge of tears.

"People will come to understand. Please don't fret. We'll have this behind us soon."

Jane nodded, looking unconvinced.

Elizabeth gave her a quick hug, then a gentle shove toward the steps. After watching Jane go up, she hurried after her aunt and uncle. She reached them in time to accept the arm her uncle offered.

Entering the large parlor on her uncle's arm, Elizabeth searched through the sea of familiar faces for Mr. Wickham. It didn't take long to spot him standing beside the refreshment table speaking with Colonel Forster. Elizabeth was grimly pleased. Wickham's choice of both location and companion couldn't be better.

"He's by the refreshment table," Elizabeth said under her breath to her uncle.

He nodded, adjusting their course.

As they crossed the room, Elizabeth tried to ignore the stunned looks. She hoped what she'd assured Jane was true; people would understand the need for their presence in Lucas Lodge tonight and not condemn them for being out so soon. She tilted up her chin, pressing her lips into a firm line. Grief laden as she was, she couldn't muster a smile.

Elizabeth knew the moment Colonel Forster saw her, for

surprise suffused his face. Mr. Wickham spun around, likely in response to the startled look Colonel Forster was giving her. Elizabeth squared her shoulders, meeting his gaze.

"Mr. Wickham, how dare you force your attentions on my niece," her Uncle Phillips roared.

Eyes turned toward them. Nearby conversations trailed off, only to resurface as startled whispers.

"I did no such thing," Mr. Wickham said.

Elizabeth watched him look at her speculatively. It was their plan he assume she was there as a substitute victim, Jane being too gentle for confrontation. Without Jane delivering it, the charge carried much less weight. They didn't wish Mr. Wickham to feel too threatened until their trap closed around him and it was too late.

"Furthermore, I should call you out for such an accusation," Mr. Wickham said.

Elizabeth did her best not to grimace at his poorly feigned outrage.

"Dueling is illegal and challenging a man who is a quarter of a century older than you and who has never fenced and never fired a pistol is an act of cowardice," her Uncle Phillips said contemptuously.

"You call me a coward and yet refuse to consider a way of proving I'm not?" Mr. Wickham spoke softly, his eyes darting about at the growing ring of onlookers.

Elizabeth would not let him get away with confining this confrontation to the people who were close. Wanting the whole room to hear, she mustered a loud voice. "I saw the attack. Surely, my sister's grief would be reason enough not to grab her and kiss her, but not to let her go when she fought you and begged you to release her? That is not the behavior of a gentleman!"

This was met with startled gasps.

"You accuse me, but it is your sister who should decide

if my attentions were welcome. You are exaggerating what happened. I let her go when she requested it."

As they'd anticipated, he didn't deny something had happened. Mr. Darcy had assured them Mr. Wickham liked to keep his lies close to the truth, to make them more believable. Mr. Darcy truly must know Mr. Wickham as well as Elizabeth had assured Jane.

"That's not what I saw," Elizabeth said.

Out of the corner of her eye, she saw her aunt step away. She could only assume the signal to collect Jane had been given.

"Why did you see anything? I was escorting Miss Bennet on a walk, the two of us. If you'll recall, I asked you to come along." Mr. Wickham leaned toward her. "What made you follow us? Jealousy?"

"Mistrust." Elizabeth had trouble keeping smugness from her voice. Mr. Wickham was behaving just as Darcy had anticipated. She hadn't appreciated until now what a fine observer of character Mr. Darcy was, or quite how clever. "I knew you were a liar, reason enough to mistrust you."

Elizabeth's aunt stepped back into the room. She hadn't been gone long enough to have found Jane, who didn't seem to be with her. Elizabeth hoped her aunt hadn't misunderstood her role.

"You knew I was a liar? When have I ever lied?" Mr. Wickham did a commendable job of sounding offended.

"The second time we ever spoke," Elizabeth said. She worked to keep her attention on the argument, not on her aunt. If Jane was going to be late, she needed to draw out the conversation as long as she could. "You told me you would never tell of your grievance against Mr. Darcy, yet you did."

"He told me that too," an officer in the crowd called out.

"I changed my mind." Mr. Wickham shrugged, looking unimpressed. "I made no promises."

"You changed your mind about the living left to you as well, didn't you? You asked for and received three thousand pounds to give it up," she countered. Where was Jane? Jane had said she would be there, and no matter how upset she was, she would keep her word. "You lied about a good and honorable man so people would feel sorry for you and so you could exact revenge on Mr. Darcy for not giving you both the living and the money."

"That didn't happen. Did Darcy tell you that?" Mr. Wickham's voice showed strain now and his eyes looked a bit wild.

"He did, and he offered confirmation from Colonel Fitzwilliam, who was with him," Elizabeth said. They had worked upon her wording, making it misleading but not a lie. It amused Elizabeth to fight Mr. Wickham on his own terms, in the realm of near truth.

"Darcy probably told that to Colonel Fitzwilliam some time ago to explain why the living went elsewhere. Fitzwilliam wouldn't doubt Darcy's word."

"And why wouldn't he? Because Mr. Darcy has never lied to him?" Elizabeth asked sweetly. "Did you ever lie to Colonel Fitzwilliam?"

"Of course not."

"You never told him Mr. Darcy was the one who threw stones at the parson's horse, not you?"

Mr. Wickham's eyes went wide. "That…that doesn't signify. I must have been only five or six then."

"Were you? Five or six?" Elizabeth knew he was lying about his age. Mr. Darcy had stated Mr. Wickham was eleven at the time. Mr. Darcy was sure Mr. Wickham would remember the incident, as he'd been caught and punished, which was unusual.

Mr. Wickham eyed her through narrowed lids. His lips pulled up in a smile. He looked around at the watching crowd. "I've always been attracted to Miss Bennet."

She wasn't surprised Mr. Wickham had abandoned refuting her accusations about his childhood. He couldn't know which lies she would counter, being unsure what details she possessed. He'd raised his voice when he spoke of Jane, obviously deciding to include the entire room in their conversation now, though everyone was already listening. All other talk had long since stilled.

"So you say," Elizabeth countered, wondering when Jane would appear and if Mr. Darcy and Mr. Bingley could hear Mr. Wickham from where they waited.

"Anyone who's seen her can understand why," Mr. Wickham continued in his stage voice.

There were some nods among the audience.

"She was so taken with Bingley, I knew I didn't have a chance. When I was alone with her, or so I thought, I was overcome. I wanted to care for her. She is so beautiful and sweet. A gentler soul has never walked this earth."

"Which is why you thought you could force me to marry you by saying you'd compromised me?" Jane said as she entered the room, drawing every eye. "You swine! How could you attempt to take such advantage of me, and in my grief? Elizabeth didn't tell me about you because she thought you deserved a chance to improve, but I think you may be beyond reformation."

Elizabeth hadn't thought any such thing, but she didn't mind Jane's improvisation. Trust her sister to want to make her seem good, even in the midst of a scene. She would set Jane straight later by admitting Mr. Wickham's nature had slipped her mind in the wake of their family's death.

"I think I need more of an explanation from you, Wickham," Colonel Forster said, his face grim.

"These girls are clearly deranged from the tragic deaths of their family." Mr. Wickham shook his head, affecting a pitying expression. "They are exaggerating a minor incident into an attack. I kissed a pretty girl. I asked her to marry me. What is the harm?"

There were some murmurs of agreement. Elizabeth fought not to scowl at those issuing them. What harm indeed!

"And what of maligning Mr. Darcy and lying?" Forster looked unsure, glancing from Elizabeth back to Mr. Wickham.

"Lies and delusions," Mr. Wickham declared in a strident voice.

"No, they are not," said Mr. Darcy.

He strode forward, his head clearly visible above the crowd, and Elizabeth had to admit he cut a striking figure. Mr. Wickham whipped around toward the sound of his voice. As the crowd parted for Mr. Darcy and Mr. Bingley, Mr. Wickham's face turned red.

"Mr. Wickham's acceptance of the three thousand pounds was done in the presence of two witnesses, both of whom also signed the same document he signed, giving up the living," Mr. Darcy said. He came to a halt before Mr. Wickham, Mr. Bingley at his side.

"Who are these witnesses? People you paid?" Mr. Wickham sneered, but he backed away from Mr. Darcy, running a shaking had through his hair.

"My attorney and Reverend Barnes, as you well know," Mr. Darcy countered. "I do pay my attorney, but Reverend Barnes happened to be visiting. Anyone who doubts can write them. That will make it three people and a signature against one."

A low buzzing filled the room as people whispered their opinions. Elizabeth couldn't make out any individual voices, but she was sure the room was on their side now.

"Wickham, I am waiting for an explanation," Colonel Forster said, his tone hard.

Mr. Wickham looked at him, opening his mouth and closing it again, no words uttered.

"Mr. Wickham, if you apologize to Miss Bennet and admit you lied about her, I will not sue you for slander," Mr. Darcy said. "If word reaches me you ever malign any young lady, I will sue you. I may not be able to collect anything, because I believe your debts outweigh your assets, but if you ever come into money, I will see my debt is collected, even if it costs me more to collect it than it is worth. If you don't ever come into money, something tells me you don't want to garner the attentions of the court."

Mr. Wickham took another step back. He turned wide eyes on Jane. "Miss Bennet, I was wrong. I apologize."

"You lied," Mr. Bingley said through gritted teeth, echoing Elizabeth's thoughts.

"I lied." Mr. Wickham cast a fearful look at his colonel.

"And now there is the issue of your debts in Meryton," Elizabeth's Uncle Phillips said. "I believe the tally is easily more than the minimum to send you to debtors' prison. I would be happy to buy your debts and start the process."

Mr. Wickham bolted.

CHAPTER SIX

After giving Elizabeth and Miss Bennet a few days to collect themselves, Darcy and Bingley called at the Phillips to see how they were handling the aftermath of the scene at Lucas Lodge. They both looked well enough and both had ready smiles, though those were still shadowed by sorrow. Darcy liked to think Elizabeth's greeting for him was warmer than the one she offered Bingley. There could be no doubt the ones exchanged by Bingley and Miss Bennet were as enthusiastic as the subdued nature of recent events allowed.

"I should like to take a walk," Miss Bennet said once greetings were exchanged.

Darcy saw the startled look Elizabeth gave her sister. He was surprised as well. He would have thought Miss Bennet not kindly disposed toward walks for a time.

"Are you certain?" Elizabeth asked.

"I am. I should like to walk the same path as I took with Mr. Wickham."

Now even Bingley looked surprised.

"It truly is a beautiful place to walk," Miss Bennet said. "He wasn't lying about Lydia loving it there, for she'd told me the same thing. That's why I agreed to go with him." She gave Darcy a sad smile. "As you said, he fills his lies with truth to make them believable."

Darcy nodded. "He does."

"I should like to have good memories to replace the bad ones, so I won't fear walking in one of Lydia's favorite places," Miss Bennet said.

Elizabeth scrutinized her sister for a moment before nodding. "Then that is what we shall do."

Elizabeth and Miss Bennet retrieved their bonnets and the four of them set out. Miss Bennet, walking beside Bingley, seemed inclined to hurry. Darcy lengthened his stride. He was a bit startled to feel Elizabeth's hand touch his arm. He looked down to find her smiling up at him.

"It's too fine a day for such a quick pace," she murmured.

Darcy raised his eyebrows but slowed. What Elizabeth said made complete sense. It was a fine day, and he had no need to chaperone Bingley, nor to be chaperoned while with Elizabeth. In fact, as they left town, he realized this was the first time he'd been alone with her in far too long.

"Miss Elizabeth," he said, proffering his arm. "The road is less even here."

"Thank you," she said, availing herself of his support.

Her hand on his coat sleeve brought her noticeably nearer. She smelled faintly of rose petals and the promise of spring. As they walked, her skirts brushed his leg. He wanted to stop and face her so he could read her eyes. He longed to ask her if her opinion of him had altered in any encouraging way. He wondered if she'd noticed how he'd reformed himself.

"I'm glad you and Mr. Bingley found your way through the kitchen to approach from the other direction so Mr. Wickham couldn't see you until it was too late," Elizabeth said. "I never thought of you as someone who would be willing to go through a kitchen."

He affected an easy shrug, surprised her thoughts were so parallel to his own. "I am not above kitchens. Your uncle was magnificent."

"He was. I've underrated him." She glanced up at him.

"I have as well." He'd also underrated Mr. Phillips on his handling of his wife. She responded to his patience by being a better person than her deceased sister ever was.

"Thank you for all of your help. I think Jane will recover from what happened without too much difficulty."

"I believe Bingley would like to help in that recovery."

"And you will permit it?"

"I will support it."

Her eyes dropped, but he could see her smile. She gently steered him from the road and up an unused looking path. Though it wasn't strictly proper, he didn't protest. He wondered if it was the same one Wickham had taken and they would find Bingley and Miss Bennet ahead. He rather hoped not.

"Allow me to apologize to you for misjudging your family," he said.

"Then allow me to admit you did not completely misjudge them. Did you know my aunt sent a servant to summon Jane? It was a servant she knew well and knew would complete the task, but it was her one role to play, and an important one, yet she didn't see to it herself."

"I did not know, but I had wondered why she was in the room when we arrived."

"She didn't want to miss the spectacle. She's a gossip." Elizabeth sighed.

"I will admit I may not have thought much of your aunt in the past, but she played her part well. Sending the servant was almost cunning. It would have looked odd to Wickham if he'd noticed her departure."

Elizabeth laughed. "You found the good in someone in a manner worthy of Jane, Mr. Darcy."

"I shall take that as high praise."

She cast him an amused look, but it disappeared as she turned her eyes back to the path they walked. Though she engaged in light laughter and gentle smiles, Darcy could still feel the sorrow enshrouding her. He wished their relationship was of a closer nature, so he could offer her the comfort of his arms to ward off some small portion of her grief, or speak in low tones of his parents' deaths, sharing the small amount of wisdom he possessed on such matters.

"Mr. Darcy, I never apologized for misjudging you so completely and for the harshness of our final exchange in Kent."

That sounded like progress for his cause. Perhaps they were closer to him offering comfort than he'd dared hope. "Your statement yesterday is apology enough."

"My statement?"

"That I am a good and honorable man."

A blush touched her cheeks. "You are those things, as you well know. You do not need my confirmation of it."

He stopped walking. Elizabeth turned, her eyes questioning. He caught her hand in his as it slid from his arm. They were quite alone now. He couldn't hear any sounds of humanity, not even Bingley and Miss Bennet. There was only the sound of a light breeze and the trill of birds.

"Forgive me for saying as much, but you are wrong," he said. "I do need your confirmation of it. Yours more than anyone's."

Elizabeth looked up at him through luminous eyes. He reached for her other hand. She didn't protest, further raising his hopes.

"It is really too soon to say anything, I know," he said. "Yet I cannot pass this moment by. You were magnificent in your handling of Wickham, and before a room filled with people no less. Everything I have seen of you since returning to Hertfordshire only stands to confirm I was as right to propose to you as I was wrong in how I went about it. I was also egregiously wrong in my expectations as to your answer. My feelings...well, my feelings have changed." He took in the hurt surprise in her expression and hurried on, realizing he was once again making a poor showing. "That is, I love you just as much, or more, but I admire you so much more. Please don't be upset about the impropriety of proposing so soon after your family's deaths. I can wait a long time for an answer."

She stared at him. Tears shimmered in her eyes. His heart stopped mid-beat. He'd frightened her when he said his feelings had changed. He hadn't meant to, but maybe her sorrow had clarified to her that she wanted his love, or maybe his blundering words had driven her further away. He almost dreaded learning which, for fear of the latter.

"You don't need to wait," she finally said. A smile curved her lips. "I was a fool to believe Mr. Wickham, but I would be a greater fool by far if I let you get away."

Darcy pulled her to him, their lips meeting. Throwing propriety to the wind, he reveled in her kisses, not caring that anyone might come up the path. He'd waited too long to hold her to stop now. He wanted desperately to kiss away her sorrow.

"Ahem."

Darcy recognized the voice as Bingley's. Reluctantly, he set Elizabeth away from him, but took one of her hands in his. "Bingley," he said, affecting a cool tone. From the corner of his eye, he could see the redness sufficing Elizabeth's face, but he could also glimpse her smile.

"Darcy," Bingley said, looking amused.

Darcy noticed Bingley was holding Miss Bennet's hand. She, too, was blushing. Taking in her slightly disheveled appearance, he didn't think her coloring was entirely due to stumbling upon him kissing her sister. It appeared Miss Bennet had created some of the pleasant memories she'd sought. "Time to return to town?" Darcy suggested.

"I imagine so," Bingley said.

"Yes," Elizabeth said. "I think we'd best. I believe Uncle Phillips has a busy evening ahead of him. We wouldn't want to add to that by worrying him with tardiness."

Pleased he now had a lifetime to ensure Elizabeth's happiness, Darcy settled her hand on his arm and led the way back to Meryton.

EPILOGUE

Mr. Phillips sat down at his desk to write Mr. Gardiner.

My Dear Brother Edward,

Do not be alarmed at receiving another letter from me. I have no tragedy to report, unless you consider it a tragedy Jane and Elizabeth won't be with you in London this coming winter. Jane is engaged to Mr. Bingley. You've heard about him and I'm sure you will approve of him when you meet him. Elizabeth surprised all of us by accepting a proposal from Mr. Darcy.

Mr. Phillips put down his pen. He wasn't certain how much Mr. Gardiner knew about Darcy and needed to think on how to describe him favorably but not fawningly. He picked up his glass of port and took a sip, reflecting on the past few days.

Yes, Elizabeth had surprised them all. If he was possessed of any level of perception, and his wife was to be believed, Elizabeth hadn't cared for Mr. Darcy when he'd first been in Hertfordshire. Now she'd enthusiastically agreed to a proposal from him, and Darcy was talking about inviting him and his wife to Pemberley. It amused Mr. Phillips to think of how his wife would behave in Darcy's grand home, but he would visit them because he would miss Elizabeth. Fortunately, he would be able to see Jane often.

Mr. Phillips was pleased he knew his niece well enough

to see her affection for Darcy was genuine. Although he could see the glowing happiness of both his nieces oftentimes disappeared when they remembered their families, he hoped time and love would help heal their grief. He smiled, knowing both his nieces were wedding good men.

Good men, but ones not overly familiar with the law. Mr. Phillips was moderately sure Mr. Darcy had no notion of how short the statute of limitations was for slander. With any luck, Mr. Wickham's education was similarly lacking. He wondered if he should advise Mr. Bingley to buy up Wickham's debts, in case he ever needed insurance against Wickham slandering Jane's name.

Perhaps it would be unnecessary, since reports had it Mr. Wickham had left Lucas Lodge to go immediately to his quarters and gather his possessions. There was even a rumor that another officer had a small stash of money that had disappeared. Wickham had also disappeared, and Mr. Phillips doubted they would hear from him again. He was probably trying to get used to another name, even though the theft could likely never be proven. The debts could be, and that was enough.

Mr. Phillips took another sip of port, his attention wandering over the papers arranged on his desk. Aside from the letter, he had another task to attend to: drawing up a new will. There was less money than before. The five thousand pounds he'd added to Mr. Bennet's meager savings had decreased his worth.

Not by much, however. In spite of them finding wealthy husbands, he was still pleased with the deception he'd practiced in increasing Jane's and Elizabeth's funds. He hadn't wanted his nieces to go through life feeling bitter toward their father. Let them believe he'd provided for them. No one ever need learn he hadn't.

Not even Mrs. Phillips. She'd found one of his secret bank accounts, but the other two remained hidden. He recalled Mr. Bingley's sister boasting about her dowry. Her superciliousness had momentarily tempted him to allow rumor of his wealth to surface, but he'd quelled the desire. It was a pity he would never find out the reaction when his will was read, and his worth discovered.

In spite of their obvious lack of need, he was still going to will his money to his nieces. Though, he should leave something to the Gardiner children as well. Making it per stirpes, not per capita, would mean his two favorite nieces would share half of what was left.

He would put the money in trust and allow Mrs. Phillips to live off the interest but give her no way to touch the principal, since he didn't trust his wife with money. Years ago, when Mr. Phillips had taken over the law firm from old Mr. Gardiner, he'd promised he would take care of the man's daughter, and he did. It saddened Mr. Phillips they didn't have any children, but fate had compensated his pain at that loss by giving him Jane and Elizabeth. He was glad he was able to help them.

Setting his port aside, Mr. Phillips returned to writing his letter, a much happier one than the last, smiling all the while.

~ The End ~

ABOUT THE AUTHORS

Renata McMann

Renata McMann is the pen name of Teresa McCullough, someone who likes to rewrite public domain works. She is fond of thinking, "What if?" To learn more about Renata's work and collaborations, visit www.renatamcmann.com.

Summer Hanford

Starting in 2014, Summer was offered the privilege of partnering with fan fiction author Renata McMann on her well-loved *Pride and Prejudice* variations. More information on these works is available at www.renatamcmann.com.

Summer is currently partnering with McMann as well as writing solo works in Regency Romance and Epic Fantasy. She lives in the Finger Lakes Region of New York with her husband and compulsory, deliberately spoiled, cat. The newest addition to their household, an energetic setter-shepherd mix, has been trying, and failing, for six years to gain acceptance from the cat, but is adored by the humans. For more about Summer, visit www.summerhanford.com.

www.ingramcontent.com/pod-product-compliance
Lightning Source LLC
Chambersburg PA
CBHW021808150726
47989CB00004B/1824